P9-CFQ-177

Into the Deep Forest

WITH HENRY DAVID THOREAU

by Jim Murphy

Illustrated by Kate Kiesler

Clarion Books/New York

Clarion Books
a Houghton Mifflin Company imprint
215 Park Avenue South, New York, NY 10003

Title calligraphy by Iskra.

The illustrations for this book were executed in oil and pencil on board.
The text was set in 14/19-point Centaur.

Printed in the USA

Library of Congress Cataloging-in-Publication Data

Murphy, Jim, 1947–
Into the deep forest with Henry David Thoreau / by Jim Murphy ;
illustrated by Kate A. Kiesler.
p. cm.
ISBN 0-395-60522-9
1. Katahdin, Mount, Region (Me.)—Description and travel—Juvenile literature.
2. Thoreau, Henry David, 1817–1862—Journeys—Maine—Katahdin, Mount,
Region—Juvenile literature. I. Kiesler, Kate A. II. Title.
F27.P5M87 1995
917.41'25—dc20 94-11791
CIP
AC

HOR 10 9 8 7 6 5 4 3 2 1

To Lorraine and Jerry Murphy,
who survived the journey over Low Gap Road
and know exactly what Henry went through.
—J.M.

And to Barry,
for sharing his knowledge.
—K.K.

A Note About the Text

Henry David Thoreau made three trips into the wilderness of Maine and, in addition to his journal entries, he wrote long articles about each trip ("Ktaadn and the Maine Woods," "Chesuncook," and "The Allegash and East Branch"). Because the routes of these trips overlapped in many places, Henry was able to revisit and write about certain areas several times. Most of the text of *Into the Deep Forest* is from the journal entries and the article about his third trip, though some incidents and descriptions from his earlier visits have been used because they give a fuller sense of what he saw and felt. Changes to his original text have been kept to a minimum; longer descriptive passages have been shortened and the verb tense has been made consistent throughout. In a few cases, words have been added to smooth transitions or for clarity, and these are in brackets. Henry David Thoreau did not like his writing altered by anyone, and I have made all of these changes with great humility and care.

Henry David Thoreau

About Henry

"I think that I cannot preserve my health and spirits," Henry David Thoreau wrote in his journal, "unless I spend four hours a day . . . sauntering through the woods and over the hills and fields, absolutely free from all worldly engagements."

And so, every day for over thirty years, Henry would leave his home in Concord, Massachusetts, and stride through the surrounding swamps and brush and forest. It was only when he was away from town and the prying eyes of his neighbors that Henry felt truly free—to follow any path he chose, to study carefully what was around him, and to think any thought he wanted.

Few people meeting Henry for the first time would take him for much of a thinker. He liked to wear simple work shirts, rumpled pants, and boots that were heavily greased to keep water out. What is more, his hands were rough from years of hard work, while constant exposure to sun, rain, and icy winds had left his face tanned and deeply lined. But if his appearance was unremarkable, his mind was not. In fact, Henry David Thoreau is now considered one of the great American writers, philosophers, and naturalists of the nineteenth century.

Henry's fascination with the countryside began at a very early age. He was born on his grandmother's farm in 1817 and lived there happily, surrounded by farm animals and fields and cold mountain streams. When his family moved to Concord, his parents often took Henry and his older brother and sister on long hikes and picnics in the woods outside of town. There, his mother encouraged Henry's love of nature and even taught him how to stay very still so he could hear the songs of birds. As he grew older, his brother, John, showed Henry how to tell when an animal was near and how to follow its trail.

Though he spent a great deal of time perfecting his outdoor skills, Henry also managed to be a good student. Shortly after he turned sixteen, Henry entered Harvard College. It was during his second year there that he began noting what he saw and thought in his journal, a habit Henry maintained faithfully until he died in 1862.

While at Harvard, Henry happened to meet one of his Concord neighbors, Ralph Waldo Emerson. Emerson was already a famous writer and philosopher as well as the leader of a group of fellow writers and philosophers called the Transcendentalists. Emerson liked Henry and appreciated his keen mind, so he encouraged the young man to study and pursue his ideals.

Shortly after his graduation, Henry joined his brother in opening a school. One of their educational innovations was taking students on "field trips" to study plants and animals near the school. Sadly, they were forced to close the school when John became ill.

After this, Henry gave up on finding a full-time job so he would have more time to study nature and write. To earn money, he became a part-time handyman, doing anything from chopping wood, surveying, and painting houses to shoveling manure out of stables. Henry also worked in his father's pencil factory and is credited with inventing an improved way to insert graphite into the pencil shaft.

Henry did a great many chores for Emerson and even lived with the Emerson family for several years. While there he met the other members of the Transcendentalist Club and helped Emerson edit their writings.

Being near Emerson and his literary friends fueled Henry's desire to write, so he borrowed some land that Emerson owned on Walden Pond, built a tiny cabin, and lived there by himself for two years. He managed to complete a book about a journey he and his brother had taken (*A Week on the Concord and Merrimack Rivers*) as well as keep his journal and produce several essays. But Henry also went there to see if he could live a simple life, one that would not cost much money and would not require a steady income. He felt that Americans were much too absorbed with making money and buying things, and not concerned enough about how they lived their lives or with appreciating the world around them.

In addition, Henry kept precise records of the weather, the water level of the pond, the kinds of fish that lived there, and the comings and goings of the wildlife in the surrounding forest. He even brought up underwater plants in order to identify them. Henry was the first American to study a lake ecosystem in such an organized and detailed way.

Eventually, Henry would describe his experiment in simple living in a book called *Walden, or Life in the Woods. Walden* is one of the most widely read American classics and has influenced such writers as Leo Tolstoy, W. B. Yeats, and Ernest Hemingway.

Henry's stay at Walden Pond was a peaceful retreat for the most part, but it did have at least one dramatic moment. To protest the Mexican War and the federal government's extension of slavery, Henry refused to pay his taxes. As a result, Henry was arrested by the local sheriff and had to spend a night in jail. Henry felt that citizens not only had a right to protest when their government did anything wrong, they had an obligation to express their opinion. His most powerful essay, *Civil Disobedience,* would describe the incident and, years later, be used by people such as Mahatma Gandhi and Martin Luther King, Jr., in their struggles for freedom and civil rights.

While most of Henry's life was spent in and around Concord, he did manage several longer journeys to places like Cape Cod (1849), Canada (1850), and Long Island, New York (1850). He also made three hiking/canoe trips into the wilderness of Maine (in 1846, 1853, and 1857). These trips were sometimes dangerous and always exhausting, yet Henry still managed to take careful notes along the way.

What follows is an account of one of these journeys into the Maine woods. Henry had two traveling companions on this trip. One was a friend from Concord, Edward Hoar. The other was Joe Polis, their Native American guide. Their destination was the second-highest mountain in Maine, Mount Ktaadn (its name is now spelled Mount Katahdin). Actually, it was Edward who wanted to climb Ktaadn. Henry had been to Ktaadn already, but agreed to go again if they took a long, roundabout route that would let them travel on a number of rivers and lakes and streams. For Henry, the real object of the journey was to see and experience as much of nature as he could along the way.

And Henry saw a great deal. A friend of his observed that it was as if "nature, in return for [Henry's] love, seems to adopt him as her especial child; and shows him secrets which few others are allowed to witness."

A COLD MIST CLINGS to Moosehead Lake this September morning, but Henry hardly notices it. He is eager to get the birch-bark canoe launched. His friend Edward and their guide, Joe, help him secure the supplies until "the canoe is as closely packed as a market basket." Then they push the canoe away from the shore.

The lake is calm and smooth, and the gentle sound of the paddles dipping into the deep green water helps Henry relax. After being cooped up in Concord, he is escaping its crowds and clatter at last. "We live thick and are in each other's way, and I think that we thus lose some respect for one another. . . . [But then] I leave the towns behind, and life becomes gradually more tolerable, if not even glorious."

Henry searches for Mount Ktaadn. It is somewhere off in the distance, he knows, but thick gray clouds block his view.

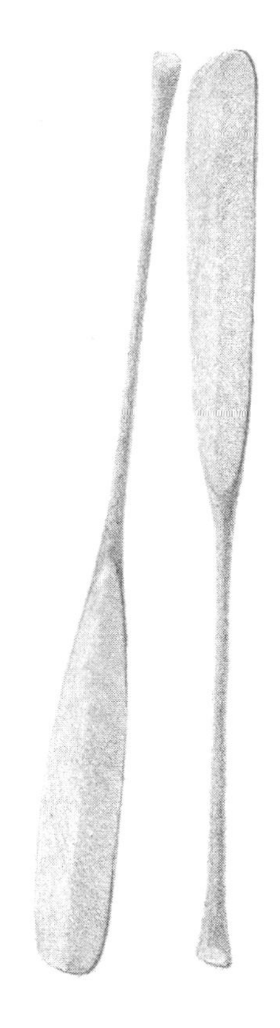

Henry's oars

THEY GLIDE EFFORTLESSLY for many hours. As he paddles, Henry hears the distinct call of a kingfisher, then sees a lake trout break the surface of the water. A pair of ducks skim the water searching for a meal. So much is happening that it is hard for Henry to see and hear it all.

a pair of ducks

The wind increases and foamy waves slap at the canoe. "A very little wind on these broad lakes raises a sea which will swamp a canoe. . . . Before you think of it, a wave will creep up the side of the canoe and fill your lap, like a monster deliberately covering you with its slime before it swallows you."

The three men struggle to keep the canoe from tipping over, all the while searching for the Penobscot River. Finally, they spot the mouth of the river and turn the canoe into it.

belted kingfisher

PADDLING IS MUCH EASIER on the river, so Henry leans back to study the woods surrounding them. In his journal, he lists the fifteen types of trees he sees. Then he adds, "The solid and well-defined fir-tops, like sharp and regular spear-heads, black against the sky, give a peculiar, dark, and sombre look to the forest."

The riverbank rises up seven or eight feet on both sides. Red maples lean out across the water, their knobby roots barely holding on to the dirt. The canoe drifts near them, and Henry is excited to see animal tracks.

"The moose tracks are quite numerous and fresh here. We notice in a great many places narrow and well-trodden paths by which they had come down to the river, and where they had slid on the steep and clayey bank. . . ."

Joe thinks the moose might still be near, so the three men decide to stay in the canoe and look for them.

red maple

THEIR SEARCH TAKES THEM up a very narrow stream to a small meadow. The meadow is still and quiet. Nothing moves until "I hear a crackling deep in the alders, and turn Joe's attention to it."

alder

Joe stops the canoe, then begins paddling backward quietly. "We had reached thus half a dozen rods, when we suddenly spy two moose standing just on the edge of the open part of the meadow which we had passed, not more than six or seven rods distant, looking round the alders at us."

One of the moose is a large female. Beside her is her one-year-old calf. Henry is amazed by their size, but he is also impressed by their peaceful manner. "They make me think of great frightened rabbits, with their long ears and half-inquisitive, half-frightened looks. . . ."

Moose and men stare at one another for a very long time. Then the moose turn and bound into the cover of the trees.

AFTER THIS ENCOUNTER, the men find a dry place and set up camp. "There is now a little fog on the water, though it is a fine, clear night above. There are very few sounds to break the stillness of the forest. Several times we hear the hooting of a great horned-owl. . . ."

great horned owl

The fire crackles and pops, sending sparks into the air like fireworks. Henry remembers the moose and is happy he had a chance to study them close up. Yet, the fact that they stood still for so long is why thousands of them are shot every year by hunters.

"This hunting of the moose merely for the satisfaction of killing him, is too much like going out by night to some wood-side pasture and shooting your neighbor's horses. These are God's own horses, poor timid creatures. . . ."

Just before he falls asleep, Henry adds another thought to his journal. "Every creature is better alive than dead, men and moose and pine-trees, and he who understands it aright will rather preserve its life than destroy it."

THE SINGING OF white-throated sparrows wakes Henry early the next day, and soon he and his companions have the canoe in the water. Traveling is easy at first, but then tree roots and rocks scrape the bottom of the canoe. They will have to land and "carry over" everything until they find deeper water.

Henry's compass

Henry and Edward divide the supplies into two bundles and tie each to a paddle. Meanwhile, Joe lifts the canoe and balances it upside down on his head. He tells Henry and Edward to follow his footprints, then he hurries off.

At first, it is very easy to follow Joe. But when the ground grows damp and a thick carpet of moss covers everything, the footprints disappear. A few more steps and their feet sink into muddy water.

Edward suggests that they go back to find another path, but Henry doesn't want to give up. Not yet, anyway. He's sure he can figure out where to go by using his compass.

DESPITE BEING LOST in a mucky swamp, Henry still makes notes about what he sees. On a small hill, he finds round-leafed orchids. Farther along, there are swamp gooseberries and dwarf raspberries.

swamp gooseberries

Deeper and deeper into the swamp they go. When a red squirrel chatters angrily at them, Henry writes, "It must have a solitary time in that dark evergreen forest, where there is so little life. . . . I wonder how he could call any particular tree there his home; and yet he would run up the stem of one out of the myriads, as if it is an old road to him."

The water is up to their hips in places and many times they have to climb over fallen tree trunks. The swamp is so wild that Henry wonders if a hungry bear might be nearby. Then he realizes his mistake.

dwarf raspberries

"When you get fairly deep into the middle of one of these grim forests, you are surprised to find that the larger inhabitants are not at home commonly, but have left only a puny red squirrel to bark at you. . . . A howling wilderness does not howl; it is the imagination of the traveler that does the howling."

THE SUN BEGINS TO SET and gloomy shadows fill the swamp. Henry worries about where they will spend the night. Should they turn around or should they continue? Henry is trying to figure out what to do when their feet touch firm, dry ground. They are relieved to be out of the swamp and even happier when they meet up with Joe, who takes them to that night's camp.

"In the middle of the night, we hear the voice of the loon, loud and distinct, from far over the lake. It is a very wild sound, quite in keeping with the place and circumstances of the traveler. . . . I could lie awake for hours listening to it, it is so thrilling."

But the fire is warm and the struggle through the swamp has left Henry exhausted. He turns over and falls asleep quickly.

loons

THE NEXT DAY DAWNS so clear that Henry can see Mount Ktaadn twenty miles away. Before long they have located a stream that leads to the mountain.

The stream is not very deep, and they must stop many times to carry over the canoe and supplies. During one carry over, Henry meets a short, sunburned hunter who has been alone in the woods for a month. Henry envies the man's freedom. "How much more respectable is the life of the solitary pioneer in these, or any woods,—having real difficulties, not of his own creation, drawing his subsistence directly from nature,—than the hapless multitudes who . . . are thrown out of employment by hard times!"

Down the path, Henry discovers a brightly colored billboard pasted to a pine tree. It is an advertisement for a Boston clothing store. "This should be recorded among the advantages of this mode of advertising, that even the bears and wolves, moose, deer, otter, and beaver may learn where they can fit themselves according to the latest fashion . . . or, at least, recover some of their own lost garments."

clothing advertisement

DURING A THIRD carry over, the path becomes rough and hilly. The lush forest suddenly ends, and Henry is startled to enter a vast area of burned trees.

"This burnt land is an exceedingly wild and desolate region. . . . It is covered with charred trunks, either prostrate or standing, which crock our clothes and hands, and we could not easily have distinguished a bear there by his color. Sometimes we cross a rocky ravine fifty feet wide, on a fallen trunk; and there are great fields of fire-weed on all sides, the most extensive that I ever saw, which present great masses of pink."

The burned area stretches for almost four miles, and Henry can only guess how the fire started. Lightning might have hit a tree; it is also possible that a careless hunter left his fire unattended.

A little way along, they come upon a series of huge slate rocks that stick out of the ground at sharp angles. The three men wind their way around the rocks, each taking the route he feels is the easiest, until they come to a small lake where they camp.

fireweed

SOMETIME IN THE MIDDLE of the night a dream wakes Henry. He is restless, so he decides to catch some fish for breakfast. He makes his way through the inky black woods to the water. "At night the general stillness is more impressive than any sound, but occasionally you hear the note of an owl farther or nearer in the woods, and if near a lake, the semi-human cry of the loons. . . ."

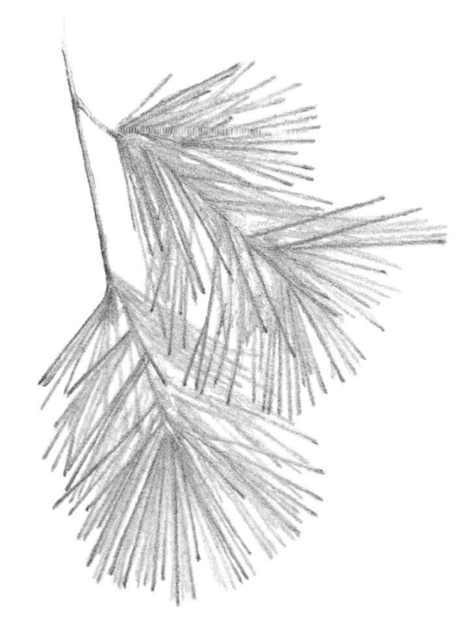

white pine bough

Stars fill the sky and the moonlight is so bright he can see Ktaadn in the distance. With luck, they will reach the mountain the next day. He baits his hook, casts it into the quiet water, and waits patiently for the first trout to strike.

Darkness slowly fades into daylight. A hasty fish breakfast is eaten, and then the canoe is launched again. They dig their paddles in, and the canoe rushes across the lake and into the next stream.

"It was very exhilarating . . . coasting down this inclined mirror, which was now and then gently winding, down a mountain, indeed, between two evergreen forests, edged with lofty dead white-pines, sometimes slanted over the stream. . . ."

AT THREE O'CLOCK they are as close to Ktaadn as they can get in the canoe. The rest of the trip will be on foot.

They set off through a tangled growth of young trees and cross a fast-moving stream. Henry notices that the ground on the other side is covered with animal tracks—mostly bear, rabbit, and moose.

For an hour they hike uphill with no view of the mountain. "At length we reach an elevation sufficiently bare to afford a view of the summit, still distant and blue, almost as if retreating from us. A torrent, which proves to be the same we had crossed, is seen tumbling down in front, literally from out of the clouds. But this glimpse at our whereabouts is soon lost, and we are buried in the woods again."

Late in the afternoon, they make camp just below the waterfall. Clouds have moved in to cover the mountain and a steady breeze stirs the trees. Edward and Joe build a fire, but Henry wants to climb to the top before night.

animal tracks (moose, bear, rabbit)

A FEW TREES GROW above the camp and Henry uses them to haul himself up huge, gray boulders. "And I mean to lay some emphasis on this word *up*,—pulling myself up the side of the perpendicular falls of twenty or thirty feet, by the roots of firs and birches. . . ."

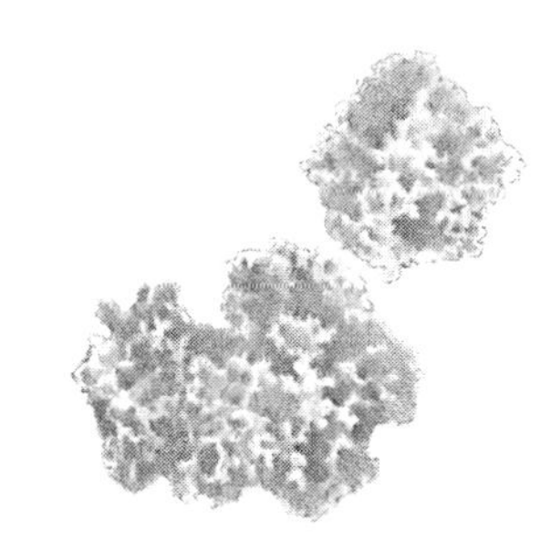

lichen

After a while, all plants disappear. "The mountain seems a vast aggregation of loose rock, as if it had rained rocks, and they lay as they fell on the mountain sides . . . leaning on each other, all rocking-stones. . . ."

A cold wind pushes mist into Henry's eyes, making it hard to see, and the lichen-covered rocks are damp and slick. Only when there are no more rocks to climb does Henry know he has reached the top of Ktaadn, 5300 feet up.

He turns to study the view, but the clouds are too thick. "I am deep within the hostile ranks of the clouds, and all objects are obscured by them. . . . It is like sitting in a chimney and waiting for the smoke to blow away."

Henry would like to stay until the clouds clear, but the temperature is dropping. Disappointed and shivering, he begins climbing down.

HE HASN'T GONE very far when the mist swirls and thins. The scene opens before him.

"I can overlook the country for hundreds of miles. . . . It is a country full of evergreen trees, of mossy silver birches and watery maples, the ground dotted with small, red berries, and strewn with damp and moss-grown rocks,—a country with innumerable lakes and rapid streams, peopled with trout, salmon, shad, and pickerel, and other fishes; the forest resounding with the note of the chickadee, the blue-jay, and the woodpecker, the scream of the fish-hawk and the eagle, the laugh of the loon . . . ; at night, with the hooting of owls and the howling of wolves. . . ."

white pine

Surrounded by all of this, it is hard for Henry to believe that any crowded cities or smoky factories exist at all beyond the vast forest.

The view lasts only a few seconds before the wind shifts and the clouds close in again. Still, Henry is more than satisfied. He has made the long trip into the deep forest and seen and experienced many extraordinary things. For Henry his journey is complete.